important decision **11**

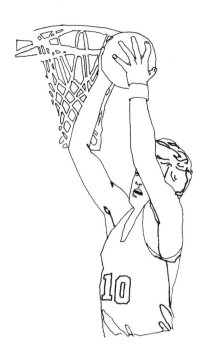

important
decision

by Paul J. Deegan
illustrated by Harold Henriksen

AMECUS STREET, MANKATO, MINNESOTA

Published by Amecus Street, 123 South Broad Street, P.O. Box 113, Mankato, Minnesota 56001.
Copyright © 1975 by Amecus Street. International copyright reserved in all countries.
No part of this book may be reproduced in any form without written permission from the publisher.
Printed in the United States. Disbributed by Childrens Press, 1224 West Van Buren Street,
Chicago, Illinois 60607.
Library of Congress Number: 74-14514   ISBN: 0-87191-401-8
Library of Congress Cataloging in Publication Data

Deegan, Paul J   1937-
The important decision.
SUMMARY: Eighth-grader Dan Murphy finds securing a starting position on
the basketball team more difficult than he anticipated.
[1. Basketball—Fiction] I. Henriksen, Harold, illus. II. Title.
PZ7.D359Im   [Fic]   74-14514   ISBN 0-87191-401-8

F
D

Dan Murphy pulled up his coat collar. The cold wind stung. It was almost dark, and there were still eight blocks to walk before he reached home. The wind and the dampness made him shudder. "Perhaps it'll be snowing by morning," he thought.

Thinking about the weather was better than thinking about the basketball practice he had finished a few minutes ago. It had been a long afternoon for Dan, an eighth grader at Oakdale Elementary School.

He had been looking forward to the basketball season for weeks. He had begun thinking about it even in the summer. This was his fourth year of playing on an organized team. It would also be a very important year.

Dan knew that only the best players on the six eighth-grade teams in Pinetown would have a chance to play in the high school program the following year. He desperately wanted to be among those who played. A few more afternoons like today, though, and he might not even play for Oakdale.

Dan was becoming a good shooter. He wasn't the quickest boy and had to work harder than some of his teammates at certain parts of the game. Defense was one. Delivering a pass and moving on offense were others.

Dan had known he would have to concentrate on his weaknesses. Maybe, he wondered as he walked in the cold, he hadn't realized how much. At 6 feet he was taller than most of his classmates. In earlier grades, he had played because of his size. The fact that he could shoot well hadn't hurt either.

During the practices so far this year, however, it was obvious that boys like Ron Dale and George Hanson, who were smaller than Dan but much quicker, were going to be tougher competition.

Today Ron had picked off passes when Dan had reacted slowly in making the pass. George had stolen the ball from him once when Dan hesitated after stopping his dribble, unsure of whether to shoot or pass.

Dan had also been a couple of steps slow two or three times when making a break off a set pattern. This had not escaped the attention of the coach, John Hook. Mr. Hook had stopped the play once. "Murphy," he had said, "you had a clear path to the basket if you had started your move on time."

Dan knew that his future basketball success at Kennedy High School depended not only on making the starting five this year but on having a good season. Tonight he was wondering whether he would even start.

Dan turned the corner onto Hanover

Street as the season's first snowflakes fell to the ground. The lights from the living room of his house were only a few doors away.

Entering the side door of the Murphy home, Dan hung up his coat and walked into the kitchen with his books. His father had just entered the room, the evening paper in his hand. Mr. Murphy had played basketball in high school and college. He had coached in kids' recreation programs since the family had moved to Pinetown five years before.

"How did it go today?" Mr. Murphy asked his son.

"Not too good, dad," Dan replied. "Things are tougher this year. After today I'd trade a couple of inches for some more speed."

"That's going to be hard to do," Mr. Murphy said with a smile. "Besides, you can learn to make up for some things that don't come easily to you by working harder at them than anybody else."

"I'm not surprised," his father continued, "that the competition is more difficult this year. Some of the other boys have grown quite a bit. All of you are going to be better every year."

"I just hope I can make the first five," Dan said. "I sure didn't help my chances any today."

"Concentrating will help, but worrying won't," Mr. Murphy said. "You never seemed to worry much before."

"I know," Dan said, "but I always knew I was good enough to play then. Now some of the guys seem to be a lot better than before."

"Well," Mr. Murphy said, "you have to figure you've improved some, too."

"Yeh, I suppose," said Dan. "It seems though that Mr. Hook expects a lot more of us than the other coaches did."

Dan's other basketball teams had been coached by volunteer fathers in the fourth and fifth grades and by teachers in the sixth and seventh grades. The first two teams had played in a city recreation program.

Sports were important to many of the people in Pinetown. A well-organized recreation program got the kids active early in basketball and several other sports. The seventh and eighth grade and the high school freshmen and junior varsity coaches took their jobs seriously. They took pride when one of the boys who had played for them went on to star on the varsity teams at Kennedy or Roosevelt High Schools.

Three of the boys who were expected to start on the Kennedy team this year had played on the eighth grade team at Oakdale. Mr. Hook, who had played on the team at nearby Central State, had finished college only two years before. The former coach at Oakdale had left the Pinetown schools to become a head coach at a high school in another town.

Dan liked Mr. Hook. He was young and enthusiastic. He seemed to know a lot about basketball. He could also explain what he wanted in a way Dan and his teammates usually understood.

Dan forgot about the day's practice after supper as he worked on a math assignment. He thought about it again after he went to bed.

"I'm just going to have to pay close

attention to what's going on," he thought to himself. "I'll try to think ahead a little bit all the time."

The next few practices went better, and Dan drew Mr. Hook's praise one afternoon. The ball had been passed to Ted Thompson playing a post position down on the baseline. As the ball was in the air, Dan noticed that the man guarding him turned slightly to follow the pass. Dan was playing the guard or point position and was on the same side of the floor as Thompson.

When he noticed his opponent look away for an instant, Dan broke toward the basket. Thompson was alert and saw that Dan was ahead of his defender, who had recovered too late. Ted fed a pass to Dan who went in for the lay-up.

"That's the way to break, Murphy," Coach Hook had called out after the basket. "Keep doing that, and you'll get a lot of easy points."

Though Dan was the second tallest boy on the team, Mr. Hook was playing him at guard. The Pinetown eighth grade coaches wanted to win games, but they also wanted to develop good high school players. Coach Hook had decided that Dan would probably grow no bigger than 6 feet, 4 inches. Mr. Murphy was only two inches over 6 feet. A 6-foot, 4-inch high school guard could be tough. He would be two to six inches taller than most of the boys he would play against. So, Mr. Hook had decided Dan should learn to play guard.

Dan was probably the best outside shot on the team anyway. That was a good start. However there were many things to learn. Dan had been a center on the fourth and fifth grade teams and had played forward and center the past two years.

One of the new things Dan had to think about as a guard was following a shot to the basket. Mr. Hook had installed the one-two-two or one-guard offense used by the Kennedy High coach. This meant that if the point man or guard followed a shot to the basket, there would likely be no one falling back on defense. So normally the point man would have to head down court quickly to cut off potential fast breaks.

Dan was a good rebounder. He had

picked up a lot of points in the past by going to the basket and putting up a missed shot. Now, he could do this only when he knew someone else was going to be able to fall back on defense. If Dan penetrated—moved inside to the basket—one of the two wing men was to move back into the point position.

The team had few full-court scrimmages. Most of the practice time was spent in smaller groups working on fundamentals. When the team did scrimmage, Dan and the other guards, Ron Dale or George Hanson, sometimes forgot to stay back. A quick basket by the other five brought a whistle from Mr. Hook.

Dan gradually picked up the new routines of playing outside on offense. On defense, he was usually matched with a forward because of his size. The eighth grade team always played man to man. The coaches thought it was necessary for young players to know man-to-man defense before learning how to play a zone.

During the next few practices, Dan kept working on staying alert. He continued to find himself waiting a second too long to make a break, but Coach Hook noticed he was concentrating harder and shouted encouragement when he moved on time.

The week before the first game of the season, Mr. Hook arranged a scrimmage with an eighth grade team from Rockville, a nearby town. There was only one junior high in Rockville, a town much smaller than Pinetown. Rockville, though, always had good high school basketball teams; so Dan and his teammates expected a good test in the scrimmage.

Dan started at the point position against Rockville. The coaches had decided to play their first teams for 15 minutes, then give the reserves some playing time. The two teams played evenly for the first five minutes. Both were hesitant, and there were numerous mistakes by each team.

Dan was being guarded by a boy several inches shorter. However, his opponent was strong and quick. The taller Oakdale team was getting more than their share of the rebounds and had just scored two fast-break baskets when Jake Tolson, who was 6 feet 2 inches, controlled the ball and whipped it down the court. Ron Dale, playing a wing position, had scored one of the baskets, Dan the other.

Rockville came down and missed another shot. The ball bounced out to Dan who passed it to Ron, heading up court. There was no break this time, and Oakdale set up their offense. The pass went into the post to Jake Tolson, the tallest Oakdale player.

Dan's defender dropped back to help out on defense against Jake. The center passed the ball back to Dan who had moved inside the free throw circle. He put the ball up before the man playing him could get back to him. The shot went down.

Six straight points. It looked as though Oakdale might control the scrimmage.

Down court came Rockville. Dan's man on defense was the same boy who was guarding Dan. The ball came to Dan's man out on the right side. Dan slid to his right, cutting off the middle to the Rockville guard. Then the Rockville player raised the ball over his head as if to pass into the lane. Dan jumped to block the pass.

It never came. As he left his feet, the speedy Rockville player moved by him and toward the basket. Ted Thompson left his man to pick up the boy who had got by Dan. The Rockville guard slipped the ball back to Ted's man, who had an easy lay-up.

"Don't leave your feet until the ball's in the air," Mr. Hook yelled from the side of the court.

Oakdale set up their offense. The ball went deep opposite Dan to Ted Thompson. Jake Tolson moved up to pick Dan's man. Dan hesitated for a second, then broke down the lane. The delay was enough for the man who had been guarding Jake to move into Dan's path. When Ted threw the ball, the Rockville center beat Dan to it. He whipped the ball down the court, and Rockville had an easy lay-up.

When Oakdale came back down court, Ron Dale moved past his man, drove inside the free throw line, and put up a jumper. Dan watched the shot and saw it was going to be too far to the left. He hustled

EASY
LAY UP

THE
FAKE

toward the basket, hoping to grab the rebound and put it back up.

However, the ball bounced off the Rockville center. He dribbled free, looked down court, and saw his teammate, the guard who had been playing Dan, all alone. Dan and both Oakdale wings had been caught inside. A long pass gave Rockville another two points.

Mr. Hook blew his whistle to stop play and sent George Hanson into the game for Dan.

As Dan walked over to where the other Oakdale players were sitting, Coach Hook motioned to him to come to where he was standing. Dan walked over, knowing what was coming.

"Dan," the coach said quietly, "you've just made three quick mistakes. Each one has given Rockville a basket. I realize you boys are only in eighth grade and will make a lot of mistakes. I don't believe in pulling a boy from a game just because he makes a mistake. But right now you're hurting us, and I want to see what George can do. Go sit for a few minutes, and I'll put you back in later."

Dan got back in the scrimmage when the first teams took the floor after the reserves had played. He made three baskets and played half the time. George Hanson also played half the remaining time.

At home that night, Mr. and Mrs. Murphy were getting ready to go out for dinner. Dan had eaten the supper his mother had prepared for him. He was putting his dishes in the dishwasher when his father walked into the kitchen to get a beer from the refrigerator.

"Did you guys beat Rockville this afternoon?" Mr. Murphy asked.

"We didn't keep score, Dad," Dan said; "but I think we won by 10 points or so. I sure fouled up a couple of times, though."

"That's not so strange," Mr. Murphy said. "You're still young, you're learning a new position, and the season's barely started."

"I know that," Dan said, "but I have to win a starting spot; and after today George has just as good a chance as I do."

"Well, Mr. Hook has to give everyone a good look," Mr. Murphy said. "It's not always easy to tell with eighth graders who might eventually be the best players. So long as you're playing as much as anybody else, I wouldn't worry too much."

Mr. Murphy left the room; and Dan went into the living room where his older sister, Sheila, and his brother, Jack, a fourth grader, were watching TV. Dan watched for a few minutes, then went to his room to read the latest issue of Sports Illustrated.

Later as he was preparing for bed, he compared himself to George Hanson. The guard spot would finally go to only one of them.

Dan thought about George's play. He was not so good a shooter as Dan and was considerably shorter. Dan's height and longer reach should make him more effective on defense, which George played with a great deal of zest but not much smoothness. George, of course, was quicker than Dan and could sometimes recover from a mistake at either end of the floor before any harm resulted.

Dan also decided that his teammate and off-the-court friend didn't seem to end up in a position to shoot very often. George could run the patterns well enough, but he really didn't expect to get a shot. He was almost always in a position to get back quickly on defense, but in doing so he seldom went to the basket.

"All the coaches talked about basketball's being a team game," Dan thought to himself. "They're right, but they still want a guy who can score . . . if he doesn't hurt the team too much in other areas."

Dan made a decision. He'd work at the things where he had made mistakes today. He would think more about his moves on defense and try to anticipate more quickly on offense. He would also try not to follow a teammate's shot if neither wingman was coming out. But most of all, he'd work at what he did best—scoring. This also happened to be what his rival, George, did least well.

During lunch hour the next day, Dan told Sam Lens about his decision. Sam was the other starting wing on the Oakdale team and a good friend.

"Makes sense to me, Dan," Sam said after listening to Dan. "Keep working at timing your breaks, though. It makes me look bad, too, if my pass doesn't get to you."

Coach Hook continued to play Dan and George about the same amount of time on the first team as Oakdale prepared for their first game against Vincent Elementary School's eighth graders.

Dan found he was more relaxed on the floor now that he had worked out what he wanted to do. If he made a mistake on offense, he didn't hesitate to work free the next time. He was scoring more often because he was concentrating harder on being in a position to score.

Coach Hook hadn't said anything about whom he was going to start at guard against Vincent. Dan hoped he would start. He was confident he could eventually win the position. Besides, the game was being played at Vincent; and if George started the game, it wouldn't be so bad because not many of their friends would be there.

The Oakdale players noticed while

warming up for the Vincent game that the Vincent players weren't very tall. Mr. Hook must have noticed this, too. When the team gathered around him just before the game, he named Ron, Ted, Jake, and Sam to start as everyone knew he would.

Then he said: "Vincent is small. I'm going to start George at the point. If they're really quick, maybe this will help us."

Dan was disappointed but didn't actually feel bad. Mr. Hook might have thought he would be hurt because he told Dan to sit next to him on the bench as the game started.

The coach had been right. Vincent was quick. One of their guards, only 5 feet, 5 inches or so, could also shoot. George Hanson was guarding him. Since Dan was likely to guard him when he got into the game, he watched the Vincent player closely.

The boy scored three baskets in the first couple of minutes. Each time he had shot from almost the same spot, several feet to the side and just inside the free throw circle. Twice he had put the ball up after a pass out from the Vincent center. The other

time he had fired after a pass from a teammate in the corner.

Coach Hook leaned toward Dan after the last basket. "Maybe that kid can shoot well from anyplace. But whoever's guarding him has to take that spot away from him."

Dan thought the coach was going to send him into the game then, but Mr. Hook said nothing more.

On the floor, Oakdale was able to work the ball inside; but Ted, Jake, and Sam were all having trouble scoring. After four minutes Oakdale was down by four points, 12-8; and Coach Hook signaled for a time-out. As the referee stopped play, the coach looked at Dan. "Report in for Hanson."

When the team gathered round Mr. Hook, he told them: "We've got to establish more offense. Dan, see whether you can't get loose for a couple baskets. And remember, don't let that guy get his spot."

After Oakdale had set up on offense, Ron Dale bounced a pass into Jake Tolson. When he started the pass, Dan, playing at the top of the circle, had taken a big step to his left. As he had hoped, his defender moved with him. Dan cut back sharply to his right and broke down the lane. Jake noticed his move and dropped the ball to him. Dan bounced it once and went up for the lay-up. The ball fell cleanly off the board through the hoop.

Dan turned and ran back down the court. As he passed the Oakdale bench, he heard Mr. Hook yell, "Nice break, Dan. Good pass, Jake."

The Vincent guard who had been scoring from outside had the ball. Dan moved up on him, and the boy passed off. At the same time he made a break toward the basket. Dan started back pedaling and dropped his head.

When he looked up again, he noticed with disgust that his man hadn't continued his break. Instead, he was moving back to his favorite shooting spot. Dan moved toward him but a return pass was already in the hands of the Vincent guard. He popped another shot. The ball hit the back rim softly and fell through the cords.

Dan shook his head, mad at himself, as he took the pass from out of bounds.

"Forget it," Sam Lens said, as he passed Dan on his way back up court. "Just keep working."

Dan and Ron passed the ball back and forth for a moment. Then Dan passed into Ted Thompson. Ted pushed the ball into the lane to Tolson. Meanwhile, Dan had faked a break into the lane and then moved to the outside and down toward Ted, who came a few steps up toward Dan to set a screen.

Dan's defender bumped lightly into Ted and stumbled momentarily. He was moving toward the sideline. Dan took two steps toward the lane, and Jake hit him with a chest-high pass. Dan went up for a jump shot. Swish! It was clean.

Vincent was still up by two, and Dan was thinking about defense as the teams returned to the other end of the court. The Vincent guard who was Dan's man was still at the time-line with the ball when Dan had turned around. "I'll set up higher this time," Dan told himself, "and make him move me to get this spot."

The Vincent guard passed off, came

over to his favorite side, and again faked a move toward the lane. This time Dan stood his ground. The Vincent player moved back toward the centerline a few steps to take a return pass. He looked inside; then decided to put the ball up. However, he was a few feet farther out from the spot where he had made his earlier shots. The ball banged off the hoop. Sam Lens jumped for the rebound and controlled the ball. He released it to Dan who had started up court but was looking for the outlet pass. Dan dribbled the ball to the center of the floor, a move to which the Pinetown boys had been introduced in the fourth grade. "Always get the ball to the center of the floor when you start a fast break," all their coaches had told them.

Sometimes they forgot. When they did, there was always a sharp reminder from the bench.

This time Dan did it correctly. Ron Dale was already ahead of him on the right side, and Ted Thompson was moving up behind him on his left. There were only two Vincent men back. Oakdale had a three-on-two break.

Dan dribbled the ball to the top of the free throw circle and toward the free throw line. Soon he had to make an important decision—keep the ball himself if he could drive to the basket or pass off to Ron or Ted. The movement of the Vincent defenders should help him make the decision.

At the free throw line, the Vincent player to Dan's right moved quickly toward him and made a swipe for the ball. Dan had slowed his dribble, drew the ball back toward his chest, and bounced a perfect pass to Ron, who had kept angling toward the basket. Ron scored easily, and the game was tied.

When Vincent moved to the attack, the sharp-shooting guard passed off right away. The ball never came back to him, and one of the Vincent forwards missed a shot from six feet.

Oakdale set up the same play off which Dan had scored the time before. Only this time when the ball came back to Dan from the post, Dan noticed something. Ted's man was moving around the screen Ted had set against Dan's defender and was ready to pick up Dan.

"Had Ted noticed this, too?" Dan wondered. In basketball, teammates often have to react together or things get messed up. Ted had noticed and had pivoted toward the basket. Dan's man had got picked again and was out of the play. Ted was alone as he wheeled toward the basket. Dan lofted a pass over the Vincent man coming up to guard him, and Ted had an easy two points.

It was a successful execution of the give and go, one of the oldest, simplest, and yet most effective maneuvers in basketball. Oakdale now had the lead, 16-14, with only 30 seconds to play in the first quarter.

"Tight defense now," Coach Hook shouted from the bench. "No easy shots."

Dan again placed himself on defense at the spot from which the Vincent guard liked to shoot. A pass inside was returned to the other Vincent guard who whipped it to Dan's man. He faked a shot, hoping to get Dan off his feet. Dan held his position. The guard dribbled toward the center. Just beyond the free throw circle, he stopped and shot a jumper. The ball was overshot and banged off the board out of bounds.

The quarter ended as Oakdale brought the ball up court.

"You're all playing well now," Coach Hook told the Oakdale team during the quarter break, "especially you, Murphy. Keep it up. You're really thinking out there. It looks as though that boy won't hurt us much if he can't set up where he wants."

George Hanson came up behind Dan and slapped him on the back. "Way to go, Dan! You really fired us up."

Oakdale opened their lead to 10 points in the second quarter and led by 18 late in the third period when Coach Hook sent George Hanson back into the game for Dan. "Good game, Dan," the coach said. Dan was tired but happy. He knew he had scored in double figures, and his team had a victory. His plan had paid off.

After the game Dan, Sam, and George made plans to go to a movie that night. It was Friday and they could celebrate the first win of the season.

While they were dressing, George had told Dan, "Looks like you won a starting spot today. I'll keep trying to take it away from you. But if you keep scoring as you did today and continue to play that kind of defense, I'm in trouble. I'll just have to make it at Kennedy as a sixth man . . . or grow six inches by next season."

Dan was pleased at what George said. He also admired George for saying it because he knew it hadn't been easy to do. He wondered whether he would have done the same if the situation had been reversed.

"Maybe two years from now you'll be a lot better than me," Dan responded. "I hope not, and I'm going to work hard to make sure it doesn't happen. But my dad says that kids can change a lot in the next few years. He says some kids who are real good in grade school never get much better, while other guys really improve."

Sam interrupted their conversation. "Ah, let's not worry about a couple years from now. Let's just win the eighth grade championship this year!"

"Yeh, then the state championship in four years," said Jake Tolson as he left the locker room.

CREATIVE EDUCATION

DAN
MURPHY
SPORTS
STORIES

56123

F   DEEGAN   **89**
D   THE IMPORTANT DECISION